MW01195677

THE TALK:
A BLACK FAMILY'S CONVERSATION ABOUT RACISM AND POLICE BRUTALITY

The Talk by Ama Karikari Yawson

Illustrations by Ashley Alcime
Graphic Design by Boris Cvekic

Published by Milestales

www.milestales.com

The Talk: A Black Family's Conversation about Racism and Police Brutality

It is time for "the talk." As much as African American parents wish that they can shelter their kids from the harsh realities of prejudice, stereotyping, racism, and police brutality, it is not feasible. The horrifying deaths of children such as Trayvon Martin, Tamir Rice, and Aiyana Stanley-Jones prove that children, no matter how young, can become victims of the horrid cancer of American racism, police brutality, and militarized police forces. There is no "talk" that can completely prevent such horrific incidents. However, parents must still attempt to awaken their children to life's challenges, prepare them for potential police encounters, and assure them that despite the obstacles of African American life, there is an abundance of hope for a brighter future and we must work to shape that better future.

This fictional story depicts a family's candid discussion of these pertinent issues in a way that is raw and powerful, yet still loving and uplifting.

Parents and educators are saying:

"Ama Karikari Yawson's ***The Talk*** is a must-read for any teacher, parent, or facilitator who seeks to understand and advance the difficult dialogue about police brutality and racism in American society. ***The Talk*** is a book of empowerment that can be useful for advocates, allies, or activists who wish to be a part of the solution and not part of the problem. Through the cogent language of poetry, the text can help move its readers from silence and inaction to discussion and engagement on issues of diversity and social justice. Masterfully, Ama integrates real-life examples of difficult dialogues about police brutality, stereotyping, profiling, racism, discrimination, and economic disenfranchisement, that display a full range of human emotions. Truly, as we strive to facilitate tough conversations about race, and police brutality, in particular, ***The Talk*** should be in every person's tool-kit of resources."

Dr. Sheilah Bobo, Educator

"The Talk by Ama Karkari Yawson is a story in poetry form which can serve as resource for parents, educators, librarians and community members to discuss police brutality, race and racial injustices with children. Ama has created a story focused on a family. A mom and dad talk to their two children about sensitive issues such as what to do if they are ever stopped by the police. The parents share history, current events, and examples of stereotyping with their children. Additionally, the parents encourage their children to be proud of their African heritage and to continue to strive for excellence. This book is a "must read" and is suitable for students in the elementary and middle school grades."

Aletta Seales, BS, MS, MLS
NYC Principal (Retired)
New York Librarians Association
New York Black Librarians Caucus Member

This book is dedicated to all those with love in their hearts who seek a better world in which people of African descent are able to live, love, and grow freely without the threats of stereotyping, racism, discrimination, political disenfranchisement, economic subordination, and police brutality.

Finally Jayden was done
with online school
Now he could find something
more fun to do

He asked his sister Jasmine
if she wanted to play
Soccer seemed like
a good game for the day

Jayden and Jasmine went to the backyard
and played soccer together
It was so great to run around
and frolic in the nice weather

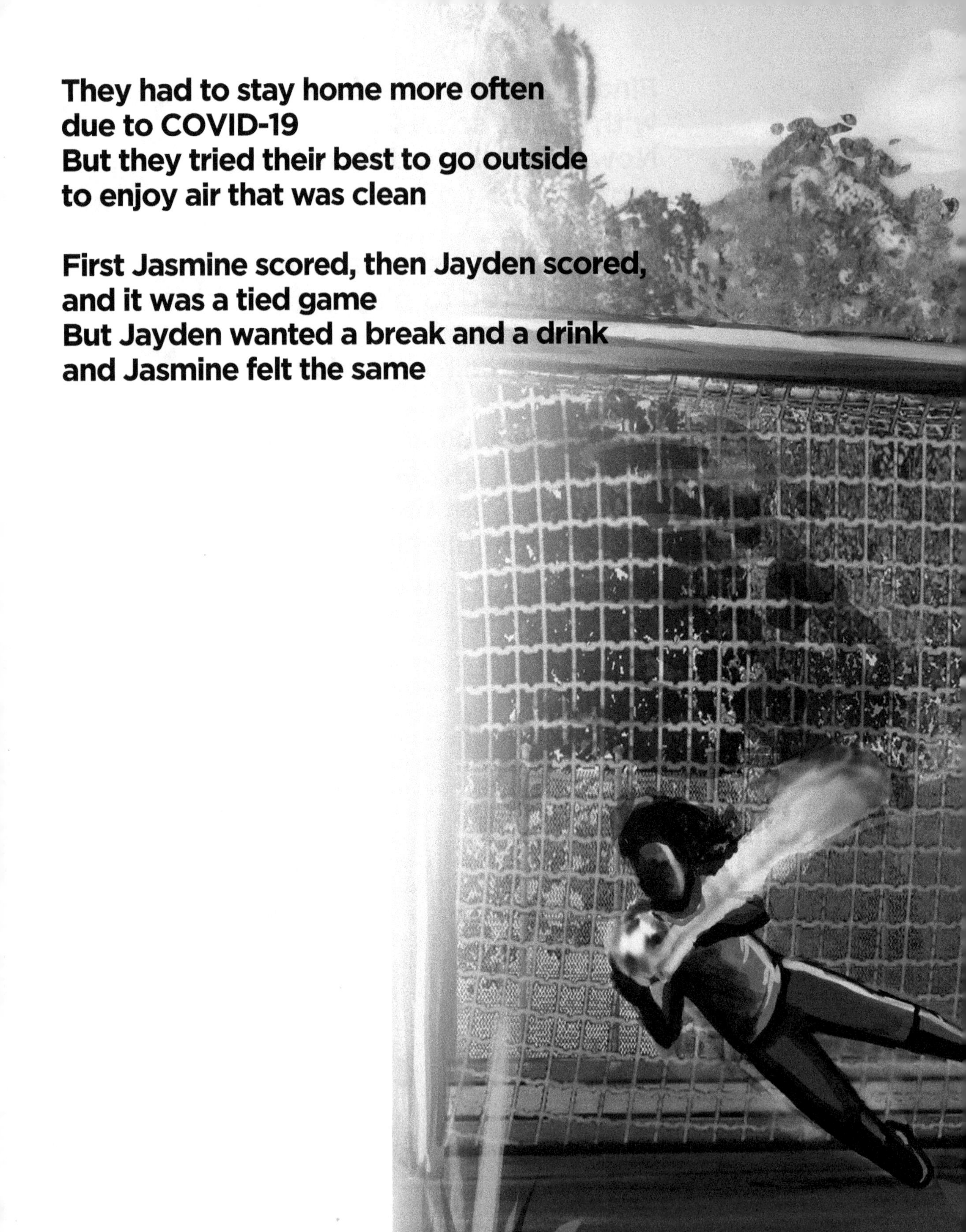

They had to stay home more often
due to COVID-19
But they tried their best to go outside
to enjoy air that was clean

First Jasmine scored, then Jayden scored,
and it was a tied game
But Jayden wanted a break and a drink
and Jasmine felt the same

They went into the kitchen for a drink of water
But their home felt heavy, there was a different aura

Jayden and Jasmine approached the living room
They walked slowly because they feared doom and gloom

Mom and Dad were hugging and crying
On the TV screen, they saw someone dying

A white police officer was choking a black man with his knee
The sight was so awful, horrendous, and painful to see

Their mother straightened up
and asked them to go back and play
But their father said, Nah, baby, I think that they should stay

They're getting older and it's time for a serious conversation
We can't shelter them from the horrible things
happening in our nation

Mom muted the TV and they all sat down in chairs
Then Mom and Dad took tissues to wipe their own tears

Mom said, You two are the most important people in our lives
You both are loved, adored, admired, and very much prized

As children of African descent, you have emerged
from a powerful hereditary line
When you keep studying your history,
you will learn that every time

You are the descendants of giants who are too numerous to name
Don't let anyone tell you differently in their attempts
to offer you shame

For example, Imhotep of Egypt was the world's greatest scientist
While Mansa Musa of the Mali Empire was the earth's wealthiest

**Queen Nzinga, Gaspar Yanga, Nat Turner,
Harriet Tubman, Toussaint L'Ouverture, and Yaa Asantewaa
made freedom their aim**

**Marcus Garvey, Kwame Nkrumah, Rosa Parks,
Malcolm X, and Dr. King did the same**

You two are loving, brilliant,
complex, and whole
human beings

You defy all of the negative
stereotypes that
we have been seeing

Since birth, Jasmine,
you have loved the stars
So at age 5 you wrote
a ten-page paper on Mars

Every time you start sharing
your scientific knowledge
I think to myself that my
little girl should already
be in college

At age 6, Jayden, you were
so saddened when
you met a homeless man
You immediately got busy
starting a lemonade stand

When you raised over
$1,000 for the
Homeless Coalition
The local chamber
of commerce offered you
an honorary position

Dad then said, While most people will truly
see you and know that you are great
There are others who will stereotype
and judge you with haste

With prejudice in their hearts and minds
They assume that they know "your kind"

They have terrible and false images
of people of African descent in their heads
They will relate to you using those images
rather than get to know you instead

Those false images were created to keep
our people subservient and oppressed
Sadly, some people choose to believe those
images and defend them with zest

Those people may assume that
you are up to no good
When, in fact, you are just jogging
in the neighborhood

They could call the police
and assume that you are robber
When you are just entering
your own home
and, in fact, you're a doctor

A man or woman might call the police
and lie that you're threatening him or her
But, in fact, you're just enjoying nature
because you're a bird watcher

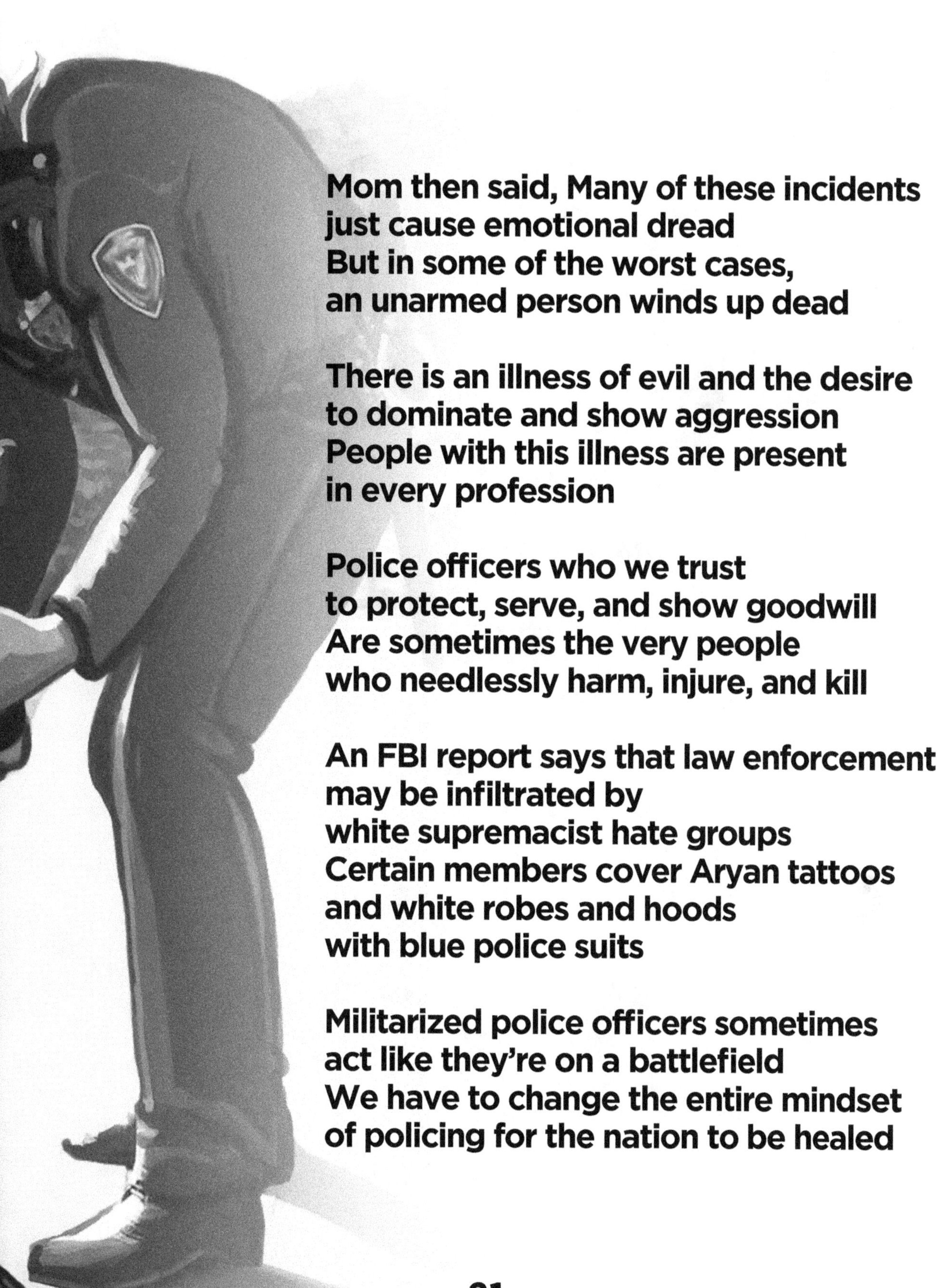

Mom then said, Many of these incidents
just cause emotional dread
But in some of the worst cases,
an unarmed person winds up dead

There is an illness of evil and the desire
to dominate and show aggression
People with this illness are present
in every profession

Police officers who we trust
to protect, serve, and show goodwill
Are sometimes the very people
who needlessly harm, injure, and kill

An FBI report says that law enforcement
may be infiltrated by
white supremacist hate groups
Certain members cover Aryan tattoos
and white robes and hoods
with blue police suits

Militarized police officers sometimes
act like they're on a battlefield
We have to change the entire mindset
of policing for the nation to be healed

You just saw on TV that a white cop
killed a black man with his knee
The black man was George Floyd and he was pleading,
I can't breathe

Many people witnessed George Floyd's painful last moans
His senseless killing was recorded on multiple cellphones

But that is just one case from a long list,
this type of thing happens so often
We proclaim Black Lives Matter because
too many black people are ending up in coffins

In some cases, a black person is just watching TV,
sleeping at home, or playing video games
Police shoot them dead before even announcing themselves
or asking civilians for their names

Sadly, the media usually assigns the victim the blame
They dig up false or irrelevant anecdotes
to tarnish his or her name

REST IN POWER

There is the case of Tamir Rice, who was just a kid
playing with a toy gun
The police asked no questions, shot him,
and now he'll never see the sun

Trayvon Martin was also a kid just walking home
after buying Skittles and iced tea
A man called him a punk and killed him,
the man wasn't even a cop, just a cop wannabe

Jayden replied, That is horrible, he was just a kid
walking with Skittles and tea
That could happen to anyone, it could happen to me

Mom answered, Yes, Aiyana Stanley-Jones
was a seven-year-old girl sleeping in bed
A bunch of police officers raided her home
and shot her dead

Jasmine exclaimed, What! It's crazy that police
could kill a little girl as she was sleeping
Mom said, It is sickening, when I first heard about it,
I spent the whole day weeping

Dad responded, We love you and we really
want you to be happy and carefree
But it is our responsibility as parents to let you know
how challenging life can be

If one day you are approached by a cop
The very first thing you should do is stop

Be calm and measured, speak slowly and clearly
It would not be the time to be loud, I mean this sincerely

Do not run, jump, or make any other quick motions
Again, you must be in complete control of your emotions

Police officers are human beings too
and they are under a lot of strain
They can get startled and accidently pull a trigger
without using their brains

So keep your hands up where the police can see them easily
You want to get out of the situation very peacefully

If you have told them your name
and they are still asking you strange questions
Tell them that you have the right to remain silent,
that is my strong suggestion

Do not hit, touch, or in any way confront the officer
Just remember his or her badge number
and later we will get a lawyer

Call us and let us know what is happening as soon as you can
We will be there to help you and come up with a plan

Jayden and Jasmine, are you listening and taking heed?
Yes, Daddy, they said because they understood him indeed.

Jayden said, I'm young, but I've felt
some of this type of stuff before
It's like when I'm just shopping
but the manager is eyeing me at the store

Jasmine chimed in, Yes, or like
when I'm at school and doing
well in my classes
But my teachers act like
I'm just like the masses

Of other kids who don't pay attention
It's like they don't want
to give me a favorable mention

Jayden responded, We hear the news
and have an idea about
what's going on out there
It's sad and scary and, Mom and Dad,
it's just not fair

BLACK
SAY HER NAME
Breonna Taylor
GEORGE FLOYD
JUSTICE
NOW!
DEFUND

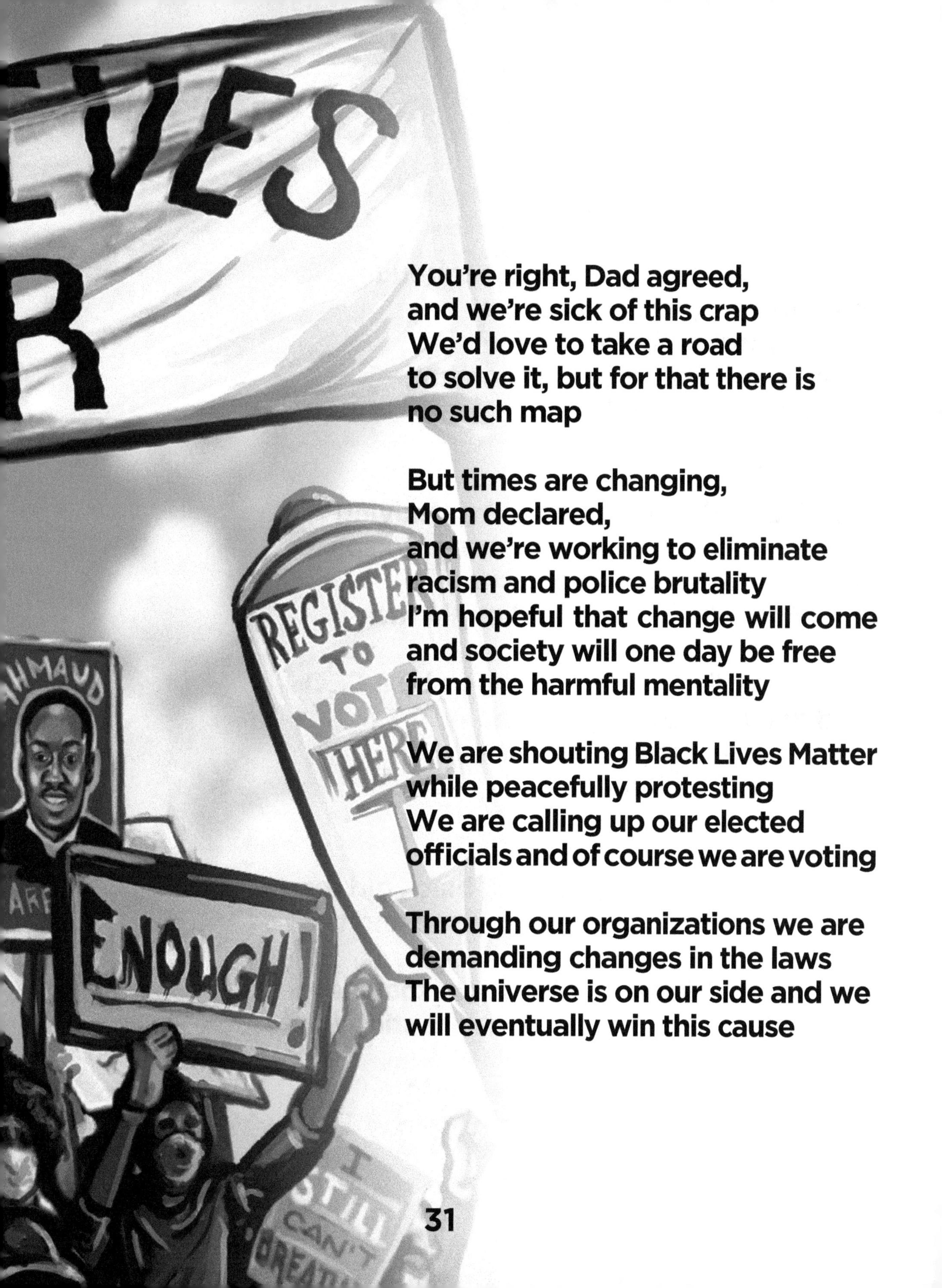

You're right, Dad agreed,
and we're sick of this crap
We'd love to take a road
to solve it, but for that there is
no such map

But times are changing,
Mom declared,
and we're working to eliminate
racism and police brutality
I'm hopeful that change will come
and society will one day be free
from the harmful mentality

We are shouting Black Lives Matter
while peacefully protesting
We are calling up our elected
officials and of course we are voting

Through our organizations we are
demanding changes in the laws
The universe is on our side and we
will eventually win this cause

You two are young and must continue
to learn, run, play, and pursue
your wildest ambitions
Your happiness, joy, improvement,
and successes provide fuel
for our parental missions

Jasmine said, I understand. I'm studying
to be like Mae Jemison and travel to space
I'm not deterred, I'll overcome
any of the challenges that I might face

Jayden replied, I'm preparing to be a CEO
and master the money game
I'm about economic freedom,
not glamour or fame

Mom rejoiced, I love it!
Show your black boy joy and black girl magic
Not everything in this world is sad and tragic

Despite the trials and tribulations that we meet
The daily victories in our lives are still sweet

We are living, loving, and growing each day
With hope, faith, and work, we are finding our way

Mom and Dad told Jayden and Jasmine
to always love themselves and to be proud of their race
Then they stood up and held out their arms for an embrace

Mom and Dad said, We love you
To which Jayden and Jasmine replied, We love you too

Glossary of Names and Terms

Aiyana Stanley-Jones (2002–2010)

Aiyana Stanley-Jones was an African American girl who loved to play. Her favorite color was pink. On May 16, 2010, she was shot dead by a police officer as she lay asleep on a sofa inside her Detroit home. Her family was the target of a SWAT-style operation in which a flashbang grenade was employed. The reality TV crew was filming the events for A&E.[1] Her death is one of the many deaths that inspired calls for more community-oriented policing and an end to police brutality.

Armed

To be armed means to have weapons and to be unarmed means to not have weapons. Many incidents of police brutality involve the killings of civilians who are unarmed and, therefore, do not represent an immediate threat to the police officers involved. Armed can also refer to having a nonweapon that provides security, efficacy, or strength such as being armed with knowledge.

Black Boy Joy

Black Boy Joy is a term of celebration for the everyday triumphs and successes of black boys and men. It evokes a spirit of carefree, happiness, and the limitless freedom to "just be" without the burdens of stereotypes surrounding black masculinity. Moreover, it acknowledges the unique beauty and strength of black boys and men.

Black Girl Magic

Black Girl Magic is a term of celebration for the everyday triumphs and successes of black girls and women. The term connotes a certain mystical and extraordinary power of black women to remain joyful despite life's challenges and to succeed at many disciplines despite the obstacles of both racism and sexism. Moreover, it refers to the unique physical beauty and undefeatable spirit of black girls and women.

Black Lives Matter

Black Lives Matter is the global movement to acknowledge the humanity, dignity, and integrity of black lives. The movement demands an end to white supremacy and the systemic racism, racial profiling, bias in law enforcement, and general inequality that produces negative and often deadly outcomes for people of African descent. The movement utilizes protests, social media campaigns, political advocacy, and various programs to fulfill its agenda. The Black Lives Matter Foundation seeks to combat acts of violence to create a space for black imagination and innovation. [2]

[1] **Rose Hackman, "'She Was Only A Baby': Last Charge Dropped in Police Raid That Killed Sleeping Detroit Child," The Guardian, January 31, 2015, https://www.theguardian.com/us-news/2015/jan/31/detroit-aiyana-stanley-jones-police-officer-cleared.**

[2] **Black Lives Matter, accessed June 8, 2020, https://blacklivesmatter.com/about/.**

COVID-19

COVID-19 is a mild-to-severe respiratory illness that is caused by a coronavirus which is transmitted chiefly by contact with infectious material (such as respiratory droplets) or with objects or surfaces contaminated by the causative virus, and is characterized especially by fever, cough, and shortness of breath and may progress to pneumonia and respiratory failure. The COVID-19 pandemic of 2019 and 2020 led to shutdowns globally, in which schools, businesses, stores, recreation centers, and other places were closed to prevent face-to-face interaction in an effort to curb the spread. Many adults were forced to work from home and many students were forced to have classes online.

Dr. King (1929–1968)

Dr. Martin Luther King Jr. was an American hero who lead the civil rights movement for racial equality. He was a minister, activist, and scholar who utilized nonviolent means including protests, boycotts, and civil obedience to advance his goal of ending segregation and promoting racial equality in the United States of America. In 1964 he won the Nobel Peace Prize for his nonviolent resistance to combat racial inequality. Right before his assassination in 1968, Dr. King was embarking on a revolutionary campaign to unite economically disadvantaged people of all races for the cause of economic justice. His goal of uniting poor people of all races continues to be relevant to this day. [3]

Gaspar Yanga (1545–?)

Reportedly of royal West African lineage, Gaspar Yanga became known as the Primer Libertador de America or "first liberator of the Americas." He was the leader of colonial Mexico's first successful uprising of enslaved Africans. He went on to establish a settlement of free people of African descent known as a palenque. His palenque was unharmed by the Spanish authorities tor almost forty years. There, African people grew food and lived a self-determined life, free to celebrate their culture and practice traditional African religion. [4]

George Floyd (1974–2020)

George Floyd was an American citizen, a father, and a security guard whose brutal killing by a Minneapolis police officers sparked global outrage after it was captured in a viral video. Mr. Floyd was unarmed and already handcuffed when a Minneapolis police officer pressed his knee and body weight against George Floyd's neck, which caused him to be unable to breathe. He said the words "I can't breathe" several times, and people who saw the scene unfold also pleaded with the officer to stop, but the officer refused to do so. Mr. Floyd's senseless death led to protests all around the world as people took to the streets to demand police reform.

Harriet Tubman (1820–1913)

Harriet Tubman, also known as Ariminta Ross, was an American heroine who escaped from slavery as a young woman and then led hundreds or thousands of enslaved Africans

[3] "Martin Luther King, Jr.," History.com, updated February 21, 2020, https://www.history.com/topics/black-history/martin-luther-king-jr.

[4] Luis Escamila, "Gaspar Yanga," Black Past, March 29, 2009, https://www.blackpast.org/global-african-history/yanga-gaspar-c-1545/.

to freedom using a complex network of safe homes known as the underground railroad. She was also an abolitionist and a Union Army nurse and spy during the American Civil War. In her later years, she took care of elderly people and orphans of African descent at the Harriet Tubman Home for Indigent Aged Negroes.

I Can't Breathe

"I can't breathe" were the words repeatedly spoken by Eric Garner in 2014 when he was killed after being put into a chokehold by a New York City police officer. Eric Garner repeatedly said, "I can't breathe," but the officer did not release Mr. Garner from the chokehold. These same three words were repeated by George Floyd in 2020 when he was also asphyxiated by a police officer. "I can't breathe" became a rallying cry for protesters and activists who demanded police reform. It was said over and over again at protests and demonstrations; images of it were printed on T-shirts and shared on social media. It represents the lack of freedom and self-determination among unarmed civilians under the threat of state-sponsored terrorism at the hands of law enforcement.

Imhotep (2667–2600 BCE)

Imhotep was an Egyptian genius with knowledge of architecture, medicine, science, mathematics, astronomy, and religion. His name means "He Who Comes in Peace" and he was eventually deified as a god of wisdom and medicine. He was the architect of the step pyramid. [5]

Kwame Nkrumah (1909–1972)

Kwame Nkrumah was the first prime minister and president of the newly independent Republic of Ghana. Kwame Nkrumah led independence efforts and Ghana (formerly the Gold Coast) became the first sub-Saharan nation to gain independence from European colonial rule. He was a graduate of Lincoln University, University of Pennsylvania, and London School of Economics. He championed the idea of a United States of Africa, which would welcome members of the African diaspora who had been taken from Africa, often in shackles, to the Americas and Europe. He was a scholar who developed Pan-African ideologies that inspired future black leaders all over the world. [6]

Mae Jemison (1956 – Present)

Mae Jemison is an American medical doctor and the first African American woman to become an astronaut. She orbited earth in the space shuttle Endeavor. She holds an undergraduate degree in chemical engineering and African American studies from Stanford University. Her medical degree is from Cornell University. Dr. Jemison has promoted health equity all around the world in regions such as West Africa, East Africa, and Southeast Asia. In 1986, she was one of fifteen candidates chosen by the National Aeronautics and Space Administration (NASA) for an astronaut training program. The applicant pool consisted of over 2,000 applicants. Dr. Jemison successfully trained and had her first space mission in 1992. Thereafter, she formed the Jemison Group to market advanced technologies. [7]

[5] Joshua J. Mark, "Imhotep," Ancient History Encyclopedia, February 16, 2016, https://www.ancient.eu/imhotep/.
[6] Ryan Hurst, "Kwame Nkrumah," Black Past, May 14, 2009, https://www.blackpast.org/global-african-history/nkrumah-kwame-1909-1972/.
[7] The Editors of Encyclopaedia Britannica, "Mae Jemison: American Physician and Astronaut," Encyclopædia Britannica, updated March 4, 2020, https://www.britannica.com/biography/Mae-Jemison.

Malcolm X / Malik El-Shabazz (1925–1965)

Malcolm X is one of the most prominent American leaders in the movement for black liberation and self-determination. During his lifetime, he was one of the most influential leaders of the Nation of Islam. Later, he broke from the Nation of Islam and became a Sunni Muslim and contextualized the African American struggle for equality in the context of global movements against colonialism and imperialism. [8]

Mansa Musa (1280–1337)

The former emperor of the ancient West African kingdom of Mali, which included the areas of present-day Mauritania, Senegal, Gambia, Guinea, Burkina Faso, Mali, Nigeria, Niger, and Chad. A gifted leader, his rulership brought peace and prosperity to the kingdom for decades. He was known as the world's wealthiest man, and during a pilgrimage to Mecca, Mansa Musa gave out so much gold that it caused the value of gold to decline in Egypt. [9]

Marcus Garvey (1887–1940)

Marcus Garvey was one of the most notable leaders of the Black Nationalist and Pan-African movement. He championed the unification of Africa and the return of black people from all over the world to the continent of Africa. To this end, he founded The Negro World newspaper to spread African diaspora news. Additionally, he founded a shipping company called the Black Star Line, which would provide transportation services for Africans all over the world who wished to return to Africa. His thought leadership centered on promoting self-love, self-determination, and economic and political independence among people of African descent. Marcus Garvey was also the founder of the Universal Negro Improvement Association. [10]

Militarized Police

Federal programs are making heavy-duty military equipment and training available to local police departments. As a result, heavily armed Special Weapons and Tactics (SWAT) teams are rushing into civilians' homes as if they are going into battle. This sharply escalates situations with civilians. In some cases, flashbang grenades that temporarily blind and deafen civilians are thrown into homes when there is a suspicion of even a small amount of drugs in the home. Such militarization sometimes has deadly consequences. Even the cases that do not result in death or injury often lead to severe trauma and create an atmosphere of fear and distrust of the police officers who are supposed to protect and serve local communities. [11]

Nat Turner (1800–1831)

Known as "The Prophet," Nat Turner was born into slavery. His master's son taught him to read and he read the Christian bible and analyzed the texts to condemn slavery.

[8] Malik Simba, "Malcolm X," Black Past, January 23, 2007, https://www.blackpast.org/african-american-history/x-malcolm-1925-1965/.
[9] Juliana Tesfu, "Musa Mansa," Black Past, June 4, 2008, https://www.blackpast.org/global-african-history/musa-mansa-1280-1337/.
[10] "Marcus Garvey, A Last Word before Incarceration," Black Past, December 10, 2011, https://www.blackpast.org/african-american-history/1923-marcus-garvey-last-word-incarceration/
[11] American Civil Liberties Union, War Comes Home: The Excessive Militarization of American Policing, June 2014, https://www.aclu.org/report/war-comes-home-excessive-militarization-american-police.

He believed that God called him to free his people from slavery. He interpreted various astrological happenings as signals to lead an uprising against slavery, and he and his followers murdered his slave master's family and fifty other whites. Eventually, he was tried, convicted, and executed for the rebellion. [12]

Oppressed

To be oppressed is to be burdened by the restraints or limitations by unjust or unfair authority or power. [13]

Police Brutality

The use of unnecessary, abundant, excessive, and or disproportionate force by the police against civilians. This may manifest through the use of harassment, intimidation, verbal abuse, physical force, tasers, instruments of torture, and/or gunfire. It may lead to significant physical and emotional harm to the victim and/or death. [14]

Prejudice

Prejudice is an unfavorable opinion formed before actually getting to know a person, place, or thing. This opinion is formed without knowledge, thought, or reason. [15]

Protesting

Protesting is the action of showing and demonstrating one's disapproval, objection, or opposition to something. [16]

Queen Nzinga (1583–1663)

Queen of the Mbundu people of modern-day Angola, she initiated a thirty-year war to prevent Portuguese domination of her people. She was able to lead troops into battle when she was in her sixties, and despite many attempts to assassinate her, she died of natural causes when she was in her eighties.

Race

Race is the idea that human beings can be categorized into different groups based on genetic physical characteristics. People who believe in race may separate people into the black race, white race, and yellow race. But genetic studies have proven that race is not a biological reality. Rather, race is a social construct that divides human beings into categories based on geographic origin, skin tone, hair texture, and facial features. Although differences in people's skin colors, hair textures, and facial features certainly exist, race is deemed a social construct because the categories of black, white , and yellow,

[12] Wilson Edward Reed, "Nat Turner," Black Past, February 12, 2007, https://www.blackpast.org/african-american-history/turner-nat-1800-1831/.
[13] Dictionary.com, s.v., "oppressed," accessed June 8, 2020, https://www.dictionary.com/browse/oppressed?s=t.
[14] Leonard Moore, "Police Brutality in the United States," Encyclopædia Britannica, updated June 4, 2020, https://www.britannica.com/topic/Police-Brutality-in-the-United-States-2064580.
[15] Dictionary.com, s.v., "prejudice," accessed June 8, 2020, https://www.dictionary.com/browse/prejudice?s=t.
[16] Dictionary.com, s.v., "protest," accessed June 8, 2020, https://www.dictionary.com/browse/protest?s=t.

for example, are arbitrary or superficial and do not account for the physical diversity of humanity. For example, some African people with albinism have white skin. People of South Asian ancestry defy traditional categories of black, white, or yellow. [17]

Racism

Racism is the belief that there are fundamental differences among people from different "racial" groups that impact achievement. This idea often leads to racial hatred and lack of equitable treatment toward people who are perceived to belong to different "races." Moreover, it has led to systems in which various institutions such as the church, government, schools, and corporations create and enforce policies and behaviors that are negative for people of certain "races."

Rosa Parks (1913–2005)

Regarded as the mother of the civil rights movement, Rosa Parks was an African American seamstress, active member of the National Association for the Advancement of Colored People (NAACP), and an activist. She became famous in 1955 when she refused to give up her seat on an Alabama bus to a white patron, in defiance of the laws of segregation. She was arrested and fined $14. This arrest led to the 381-day Montgomery boycott, in which people of African descent refused to ride buses. Instead, they walked, rode bicycles, and carpooled. In 1957, the U.S. Supreme Court declared that segregated buses were unconstitutional. She later founded an organization to teach young people about the civil rights movement called the Rosa and Raymond Parks Institute for Self-Development. [18]

Stereotype

A stereotype is a simple or standard image of a group of individuals such people of the same gender or nationality. This simple image often prevents the person holding the stereotype from being able to see members of the group as individuals with distinct personalities, behaviors, or values.

Subservient

A person who is subservient submits to the authority of another.

Tamir Rice (2002–2014)

Tamir Rice was a pleasant African American boy who enjoyed arts and sports. His young life was cut short in 2014 when, at age 12, he played with a toy gun at a park in front of a recreational center. A 911 caller told a dispatcher that a boy had a gun and that the gun might be a toy and so police should check it out. The fact that the gun might be a toy was not relayed to the two white police officers who responded to the call. Within two seconds, shots were fired at Tamir Rice. He died the next day. [19]

[17] Casey Nichols, "Rosa Parks," Black Past, November 14, 2007, https://www.blackpast.org/african-american-history/parks-rosa-1913-2005-0/.
[18] Audrey Smedley, Yasuko I. Takezawa, and Peter Wade, "Race," Encyclopædia Britannica, updated January 29, 2020, https://www.britannica.com/topic/race-human.
[19] Daudi Abe, "Tamir Elijah Rice," Black Past, July 21, 2016, https://www.blackpast.org/african-american-history/rice-tamir-elijah-2002-2014/.

Toussaint L'Ouverture (1742–1802)

Toussaint L'Ouverture is regarded as the father of the Haitian revolution. He was the leader of the only successful slave revolt in the modern era, which led to the first black republic, Haiti. Although he was born into slavery, Toussaint L'Ouverture learned to read and write in multiple languages, became a skilled horseman, and was regarded as an expert in traditional medicine. He eventually gained his freedom. However, despite being free, he joined and later led the slave uprisings that led to the emancipation of all enslaved Africans in the territory. [20]

Trayvon Martin (1995–2012)

Trayvon Martin was a curious seventeen-year-old African American boy who loved aviation and dreamed of becoming a pilot. One day, he went to the store to purchase snacks and on his way back, he was approached by a white-passing Latino neighborhood watchman in an SUV who called 911 on Trayvon Martin to report him as a suspicious person. The 911 operator instructed the neighborhood watchman to stay in his car, but those instructions were not heeded. The neighborhood watchman pursued him and fatally shot unarmed Trayvon Martin in the chest.

White Supremacist Groups

Organizations and groups that subscribe to the doctrine that white people are superior to all other groups of individuals. These groups are often also against people of Jewish faith and people who are not heterosexual. They often promote racism and hatred and sometimes commit acts of violence to intimidate non-whites, non-heterosexuals, and non-Christians.

A 2006 leaked FBI report warned that certain members of white supremacist groups have been working to infiltrate police departments.[21]

Yaa Asantewaa (1800s–1921)

A Queen Mother of the Ashanti people of modern-day Ghana, Yaa Asantewaa became the commander in chief of the Ashanti army during its fight against British conquest. When the men of the community were reluctant to engage in battle against the British, Yaa Asantewaa spoke up and said that if the men refused to fight, the women would fight, thereby challenging traditional gender roles. She remains one of Ghana's most celebrated leaders. [22]

[20] Deborah Mcnally, "Toussaint L'Ouverture," Black Past, January 18, 2018, https://www.blackpast.org/global-african-history/loverture-toussaint-1743-1803/.

[21] Maddy Crowell and Sylvia Varnham O'Regan, "Extremists Cops: How U.S. Law Enforcement is Failing to Police Itself", The Guardian, December 31, 2019, https://www.theguardian.com/us-news/2019/dec/13/how-us-law-enforcement-is-failing-to-police-itself.

[22] Racquel West, "Yaa Asantewaa,"Black Past, February 8, 2019, https://www.blackpast.org/global-african-history/yaa-asantewaa-mid-1800s-1921/.

Questions for Discussion

1. Many historical figures in African diaspora history are mentioned. Who are the figures? What did they do? Why are they significant?

2. Jayden and Jasmine's dad warns them that although they are great young people, they may sometimes experience being misjudged because of prejudice and stereotyping. What is prejudice? What is stereotyping? Do you believe that you have ever been stereotyped? Do you believe that you have ever stereotyped others?

3. Jayden and Jasmine's dad also mentions that the stereotypes are related to "false images." What are the negative false images of people of African descent that you see in the media? What are the true and positive images that you see in the media? What images do you want to see of people of African descent? How would you go about creating such images?

4. What does the phrase "Black Lives Matter" mean? There are some people who believe that this phrase is offensive. They prefer the phrase "All Lives Matter." What are your thoughts on this debate?

5. What is police brutality? What are some examples of police brutality? Why is it an issue with which all people should be concerned?

6. In May and June 2020, after the viral video of a police officer killing of George Floyd, there were news reports of looting stores and burning buildings. Many news reports contextualized the looting and burning as forms of protests. What are your thoughts on looting and burning buildings as a form of protest against police brutality or other perceived injustices?

7. The story mentions the militarized police force. What does that mean? How do you envision police interacting with people in the community?

8. Jayden and Jasmine's dad advises them on how to behave if they are ever stopped by the police. What are some of the things that he told them to do?

9. The story mentions several ways in which people can work to end police brutality. What are those methods? What are your thoughts with respect to the most effective methods for preventing police brutality?

10. What do the phrases "black boy joy" and "black girl magic" mean? How do you relate to those phrases?

Activities

1. This story uses poetry to address the social issue of police brutality. Please write a poem or story that addresses a social issue.

2. When many people attend protests, they go there with signs. Create a sign for a potential protest using recycled materials such as a cardboard box.

3. Write a letter to your local government officials. The letter should express your feelings about police brutality and racism, as well as your demands with respect to what government officials should do to eliminate police brutality.

4. Organize a discussion about racism or police brutality for your school, church, or organization.

About the Illustrator

Ashley Alcime is a visual artist who focuses on fine art and illustrations.

She conceptualizes her work as snapshots of everyday people which are conceptualized as embellished designs. She graduated from Fashion Institute of Technology with a BA in Fine Arts and Art History.

About the Author

Ama Karikari Yawson, Esq. is a sought-after diversity trainer and a successful entrepreneur in the staffing and training and development industries.

She earned a BA from Harvard University, an MBA from the Wharton School, and a JD from the University of Pennsylvania Law School. Her unique understanding of social issues, business, and the law has enabled her to become a relevant voice and sought-after speaker on issues as varied as education, diversity, cultural sensitivity, bullying, sexual violence, and personal empowerment.

In 2013, a painful experience with bullying inspired her to write her bestselling fable about difference, Sunne's Gift. Ms. Karikari Yawson became so personally invested in spreading the book's message of healing and harmony that she quit her six-figure job as a securities lawyer to become a full-time author, storyteller, and educator.

Through her company, Milestales Publishing and Education Consulting, she publishes and distributes books and lesson plans. Additionally, she facilitates life-changing workshops and training sessions that incorporate storytelling, drama, dance, history, cutting-edge psychological research, and legal analysis in order to truly propel participants toward healthier and more successful lives. Her other books include the Kwanzaa Nana Is Coming to Town series, which introduces a folkloric character to the Kwanzaa holiday. She is also the host of the WBAI 99.5 Pacifica radio show entitled How to Make it in the City. Email Ama at ama@milestales.com to book her for your next conference, assembly, professional development session, or other event. Additionally, please explore her work at https://www.facebook.com/milestales and www.milestales.com.

CPSIA information can be obtained
at www.ICGtesting.com
Printed in the USA
LVHW061448191020
669175LV00003B/158